Daisy and the Beastie

by Jane Simmons

 Little, Brown and Company
BOSTON NEW YORK LONDON

For Frejya and Oscar and
their weird parents

First Published in Great Britain in 2000 by Orchard Books

First U.S. Edition
Simmons, Jane.
Daisy and the Beastie / Jane Simmons. —1st U.S. ed.
p.   cm.
Summary: Daisy and her little brother, Pip, encounter many different animals as they look all over the farm for the Beastie from Grandpa's story.
ISBN 0-316-79661-1
[1. Duck—Fiction. 2. Domestic animals—Fiction. 3. Brothers and sisters—Fiction.]
I. Title.
PZ7.S59182Dae 2000
[E] — dc21   99-26050

10 9 8 7 6 5 4 3 2 1

SC

Printed in Singapore

Grandpa was just finishing Daisy's favorite story.
". . . they searched all over, but no one found the
Beastie!" he said.
"Coo," said Daisy.

Grandpa slowly closed his eyes and began to snore.
"Don't worry," said Daisy. "We'll find the Beastie!"
"Beastie," said Pip.

"The Beastie might be with the chickens,"
said Daisy.
"Cheep, cheep," chirped the chicks.
"Cheep," said Pip.

". . . or hiding with the geese."
"Honk! Honk!" said the goslings.
"Honk!" said Pip.

"The Beastie's not in the barn," said Daisy.
"Baaa!" said the lambs.
"Moo," said the calves.
"Moo," said Pip.

". . . or in the meadow."
"Buzz," said the bees.

There was no Beastie in the pigsty.
"Wee, wee," squealed the piglets.
"Wee," said Pip.

. . . or in the orchard.
Hoppity hop, hop!
Just then . . .

there was a noise from the shed.
"Eeooow!" it said.
"It's the Beastie!" said Daisy.
"Ooo!" said Pip.

Daisy and Pip couldn't see anything.

As they crept forward,
something rumbled,
"MEEEE . . ."

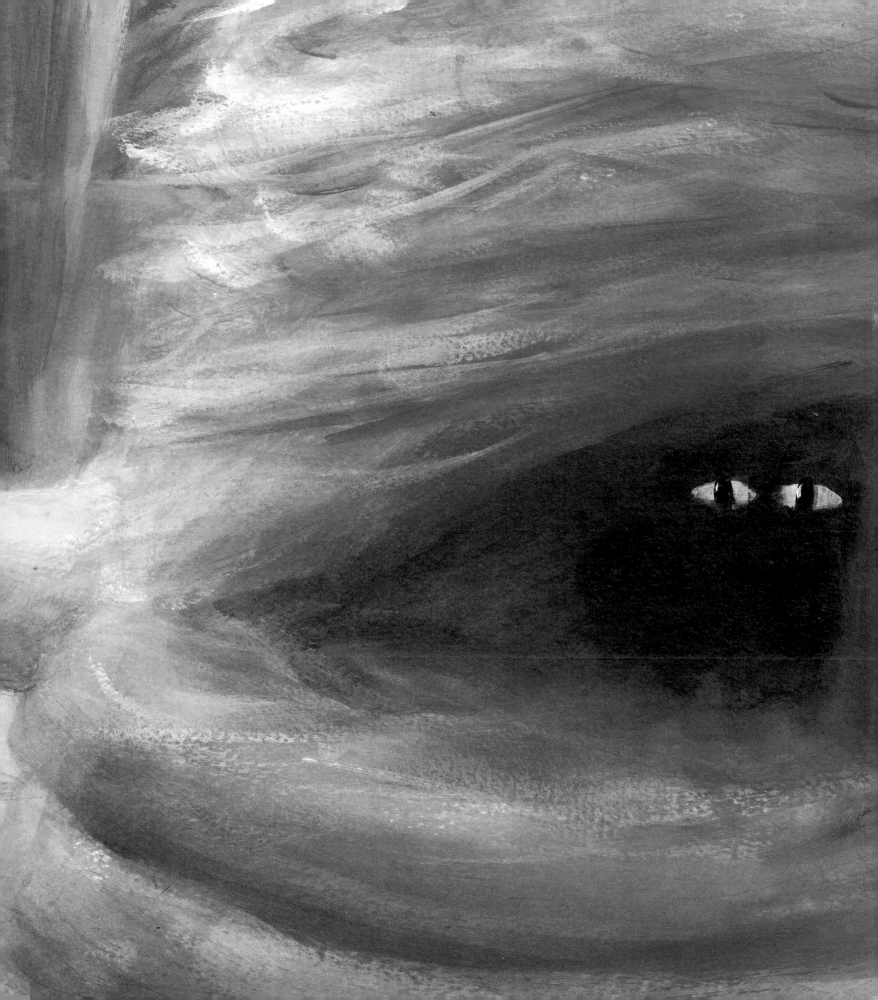

"... EEOOOW!"

"Run, Pip, run!" cried Daisy
"It's the Beastie!"

"We found the Beastie!"
"The Beastie!" said Grandpa. "Where?"
"THERE!"

"Meooow," said the kittens.
"Coo," said Daisy.
"Coo," said Pip.
Grandpa laughed . . .

and Daisy and Pip played with
the kitten beasties all day long.